DILETTANTE

A HEARTWARMING TALE OF FIVE STRANGERS WHO BECAME FRIENDS

SSHREE

CHAPTER THREE

VARIETY IS THE SPICE OF LIFE

"Prerna?" his voice short of breath, his eyes visibly shocked upon seeing Mrinalini sitting at the table reserved by his aunt. Pale and frozen in her seat, Mrinalini didn't know how to react.

The words were stuck in her mouth. Where to start? What to ask? What to say? A thousand questions.

"Mrinalini... is uhhh... my official name" her voice breaking at every word.

He sat down on the opposite chair. They stared at each other for a whole two minutes.

"So you're uhh..".

"Yes." Can he trust her to keep it a secret at work? Heck - he hasn't even trusted her with his work yet. What irony! As his mind floated around the thousand things that could go wrong Mrinalini/Prerna, whoever she is started her side of the story.

"Mrs Nila is my mom's friend. I didn't want to offend her. Thought I'd show up and tell the guy I'm not interested."

"Same here. She's my father's elder sister. My parents know about me but my aunt doesn't. I was made to go on blind dates because of her. I wanted to end it once and for all" as he started talking he became more comfortable with the atmosphere.

"You have my word. I'll just pretend this evening didn't happen." Mrinalini offered a deal.

"I'll tell my aunt we're not compatible." Mrinalini nodded as she flipped through the menu.

"I'm assuming tonight's dinner has been accounted for, can we just eat before we leave? I've travelled a long distance. "

"Done", it's the least he could do given the fact she promised not to ruin everything for him.

The calm after a storm didn't last forever. The following day, every time Mrinalini and Ritvik accidentally made eye-contact one of them would lower their head and furiously start typing on the laptop. The tension should have been so obvious to the others if not for trouble in everyone's own paradise.

The idiom *be careful what you wish for it might come true* was invented for this situation. Ritvik for months had longed to share his secret with someone outside his family, his wish had been granted only in the worst way possible.

A few desks away, Hansa who usually catches onto awkward interactions did not speak to anyone for the entire day. She would open her email inbox and read these words again and again, unable to accept the aftermath.

"Notice of Disciplinary meeting to question action raised against Mrs. Hansa Devendar"

The tragedy in discussion occurred right outside the lobby of the hotel's fourth floor when Dev and Hansa went to take a break earlier that afternoon.

Their fights usually don't last long but Hansa couldn't take it anymore she was holding onto too many secrets.

"Dev I was never rude to her. I just told here not to interfere too much. You have no idea what your mother told me!"

"I'm tired of it. You keep saying I need to trust you, but how can I trust someone who keeps secrets from me? "

In a fit of anger she lost her once coveted coolness in the process by calling Dev an "idiot" caught by paparazzi live-streaming a celebrity chef standing a few feet away.

The words still echoing in her mind, Hansa walked out of the Ethics Committee Disciplinary hearing. Five missed calls and fifteen messages later she found herself sitting in the break room sipping tea and pondering if she should apologise and tell Dev what had happened . Fate intervened on her behalf and Dev kept busy the entire afternoon in his new project.

She hadn't left after work alone for a long time now. It felt strange, walking down the corner alone and waiting for the taxi to arrive. Her mind wandered back to the argument. She had always presumed that when she stared into his eyes, it would be as radiant and attractive as it had been all those years ago, but the moment he looked at her yesterday, it was fragile and weary, a fact that made her sad.

One, two, three... she thoughtlessly cancelled her ride, continued walking.

"Do you want me to suggest some fertility treatment? Or... don't tell me you haven't thought about kids at all." Hansa felt betrayed that Dev hadn't set the expectations right with his mother. They had agreed not to have kids until she was ready.

Later that evening Dev didn't search for Hansa either, he knew she wanted space, to be alone to recharge. It was something he had learnt about her right after they started dating.

"Leaving? Or are you planning to board here for the free coffee?" Dev laughed. The weekend celebration was yet to take effect on Ritvik . A normal person would crave the drinking, music and conversation that would follow a day's work.

"I messed up my analysis and Anurag sir taunted me during the review."

"Ahh.. The usual then!" Dev chuckled settling into the lounge chair.

"You know, at my previous job, I tanked a project right before the launch date. If I can survive that, this is nothing" he smiled handing Ritvik's bag to him.

The next morning, his fingers drummed against the laptop bag. The moment he walked into the office, Ritvik looked for Dev. He was sitting at his desk, head bent over the keyboard.

Something had changed within Ritvik the previous evening, the way he felt about coming to work. Now he had Dev to look forward to...

Mrinalini has always thought Hansa as the woman who had it all — intelligence, a good partner and a nice lifestyle.

What could be wrong in Hansa's life?

CHAPTER ELEVEN

IN A NUTSHELL

Dev did not know what to make of Hansa'a revelation. So he did what he does best — run away from the problem.

He despised himself for this mentality. Yet, the two of them required space.

"You're back!" Ritvik raised his hand for a high-five as he walked into office the day he returned from his "break".

Mrinalini smiled and nodded.

"You have so many tasks on your plate" she said pointing to the table on her screen.

"Don't remind me." he shook his head opening his laptop

"Will be right back"

Just then the phone rang just then Mrinalini's phone rang, a brief moment of hesitation watched over her before she picked it up.

"Who am I talking to?"

"Mrinalini you missed your last appointment"

"Hello! Hello. Can you hear me?"

She gave Ritvik a conventional grin prior to leaving his side to speak to the voice on the phone. Some words need to be prevented from being brought to light.

"Of course, go ahead".

shaking, her face devoid of blood. But her eyes... they are RED.

D-DAY happened.

Ritvik and Mrinalini sat next to each other at the conference table preparing for the release of the most anticipated project.

The air around her tightens the grip in her throat. "We could just use a little more time. For the data to show", Ritvik urged the rest of the team to keep refreshing the screen. "Right... Right." Mrinalini utters weakly.

She's tried very hard not to show the panic swirling inside, the public humiliation she has to experience in front of strangers. The nightmare she had a few weeks back, it's all becoming very real.

The room erupts: bustling and chattering in a chaotic hubbub of annoyed complaining.

Something's wrong.

CHAPTER SEVENTEEN

SINCERER THAN THE LOVE OF FOOD

Dev turned around and locks eyes with Hansa. He stumbled a few steps as he tried to reach her hand but she shakes off his hand like it's on fire.

He closes the door behind himself.

“I didn't think it was true”, Hansa started sobbing...

”But I should have told you this long back...sorry...”

”-Slow down.” ”It's my fault. I wasn't in the right mind. Now I know, I'm wrong.” “ That's why you went on a trip. You weren't hurt, you were guilty.” ”You're like a totally different person.”

Dev's mother Lila appears next to her. “Listen my child, you are sick please get back to bed.”

“No. NO. NO” she teared up in anger and betrayal. ”You were stubborn and he called me and he asked if we could meet...And I said why...he said it was very important so I did...but I should've told you...”

”Stop Stop let me get this straight. Dev told you to talk to me?”

9 798886 297928

Printed by Libri Plureos GmbH in Hamburg,
Germany